The Horses Of Griffin Farm

By Penelope Dyan

Bellissima Publishing, LLC
Jamul, California
www.bellissimapublishing.com

Copyright © 2022 by Penny D. Weigand

All rights reserved. No part of this book may be reproduced or transmitted in any form or by any means, electronic or mechanical, including any photocopying, or recording, or by any information or storage retrieval system, without permission from the publisher and author.

ISBN 978-1-61477-598-0

First Edition

"Having dominion over all the earth's creatures carries great responsibility."

About The Author & The Book

Penelope Dyan became a teacher, an award winning published writer, a vocalist, and a mother and an attorney, all while following her dreams! And her happy life proves one hundred percent that dreams really do come true!

It was the lifelong experiences of the author, Penelope Dyan, and her great desire to do good in this world, along with her love for nature's creatures, the law, and her deep concern for others, that led to the creation of this book titled, 'The Horses Of Griffin Farm', a book with a host of characters you are certain to enjoy, and a message you should never forget.

Learn all about a girl named Janie and her hopes and dreams, and about how a horse named Cheery Day and a Dog named Pinkerton not only saved the day, but also helped Janie's dream to help the creatures of this world come true in a very special and surprising way. Meet Mrs. Carter, Janie's mother and father, and a girl named 'Hope', and learn all about life on Griffin Farm and why the name 'Griffin Farm' ended up on the farm's front gate.

Most of all, find out what it means to be given dominion over all of the creatures of this earth, and remember what Janie did.

The Horses of Griffin Farm

By Penelope Dyan

The Horses of Griffin Farm

CHAPTER ONE

A BRIGHT AND SUNNY DAY

It was a bright and sunny day, the first day of summer vacation. It was so hot the only thing you could really do was lounge around; however, for our young heroine, that was simply not an option. You see, Janie had chores to do; and come rain or come shine, whether it was a school day, a weekend, a holiday, the beginning of summer, or even Christmas day, as soon as the clock struck 8:00 AM, the chores had to be done on the farm. The chickens and the ducks had to be fed, the horses had to be put out to pasture, the horse stalls in the barns had to be shoveled clean, the pigs had to be slopped and more! And this was because, after all, this was Griffin Farm; and the whole family had to take part in the daily chores.

And the truth was that Janie did her part with a smile on her face, because raising and training horses was her dream come true, even at her tender age of thirteen years, just as it had always been the dream of her mother!

The Horses of Griffin Farm

And one thing was certain, when it came to Janie, her mother and her father and all of the animals on Griffin Farm, there was more than enough love to go around, even if life on the farm did not always go without incident. And having money was simply a way to a means, and not really something needed in abundance.

"Get up! Get up!" Janie's mother called out from the base of the stairs of their two-story farmhouse!

"I'm up!" Janie yelled, as she lay in her bed.

"You need to gather the eggs for breakfast!" Janie's mother yelled back.

"Okay! Okay!" Janie retorted in as loud a voice as she could muster.

"What a way to start the weekend," Janie mumbled, as she literally threw on her tee-shirt and bib overalls, donned her socks and her boots, and bounded down the stairs to where her mother stood waiting for her, basket in hand.

"Here's the basket for the eggs," Janie's mother said. "Your dad's already at the barn, taking the horses to the pasture!"

Janie smiled. She knew just how lucky she happened to be. And how lucky she just happened to be, had to do with more than just eating fresh eggs for breakfast every single day; and she hoped nothing bad would ever happen that would (or could) ever take the farm away from them.

And Janie's mother felt exactly the same way! And so did Janie's father! And her father felt that way because all he really wanted to do in this life was to make the dreams of his family come true!

And now, all three of them were living their dreams!

CHAPTER TWO

THE FARMER IN THE DELL

Janie's dad liked to refer to himself as 'The Farmer in the Dell', and as such he went about doing his share of the farm chores (much to Janie's great embarrassment) singing that very tune. As for the horses, they didn't seem to mind at all! In fact, there was nary a whinny to be heard from any of the horses, as the horses did all of the usual things they did during the days at Griffin Farm.

And so, the horses, the ducks, the geese, and the pigs were fed. The stalls were mucked out each day, and Janie's father planted seeds and plowed the fields to grow hay and fruits and vegetables as the family needed. And, of course, there were several dogs and cats to be fed as well. And in many, many ways every living creature on the farm was a part of their family. And life was seemingly perfect and fun. And that was because things were as they were. And the sun rose in the morning, the rooster crowed, the eggs were gathered, and Janie

The Horses of Griffin Farm

and her mother baked bread and cookies, and canned all sorts of vegetables and fruit for the human part of the family to eat.

And there was even more, as one would expect to find and to happen on a farm. But mostly (as we have already said) there was love, a lot of love. And there was a mission as well.

And that's how the story of the horses of Griffin Farm began. It began with one horse, and then it grew to many. You see, Janie and her mother and her father were out to rescue and to save all the horses of the world . . . at *least* as many as they *could* save! And it all began with one horse, and with one dream, and then two, and then three. And this time the dream had nothing to do with Janie and her mother and her father. This time it only had to do with the dream that one special horse might have. And even though it began with the saving of one horse at a time, before Janie and her mother and her father knew it, the stalls in both of the barns at Griffin Farm were nearly full.

And the work grew greater, right along with the love.

However, all was not smooth sailing, as Janie and her father and mother would find out, much to their collective excitement as well as to their collective dismay.

And so, stay tuned, and be patient, as the story of 'The Horses of Griffin Farm' unfolds, as all good stories must do. And believe, as Janie did, that even a horse can have a dream come true!

CHAPTER THREE
THE ANTS!

Janie came running into the kitchen with the basket of eggs she had just gathered.

"We have ants! We have ants!" she screamed, as she placed the basket of eggs on the kitchen counter.

"Well, they won't eat much," Janie's mother laughed, as she sprayed some cooking oil on a skillet and turned on the burner to heat up the skillet, readying the skillet for the fresh eggs.

Janie's dad walked into the kitchen, and he sat down at the kitchen table.

"How do you want your eggs this morning?" Janie's mother asked the two of them.

"Preferably cooked," Janie's dad said.

"Janie's mother rolled her eyes.

"Of course, you want them cooked," she said, not at all amused. "I'm asking how you would *like* them cooked."

The Horses of Griffin Farm

"I would like them cooked and then put on a plate," Janie's dad told her, as Janie laughed.

Janie's mother was still not amused.

"Okay, then," she said. "I'll fix the eggs sunny side up!"

"How about easy over?" Janie's dad then said. "They seem more cooked that way, somehow."

Janie's mother sighed. She wasn't much of a kidder.

"We've got ants!" Janie told her dad, changing the subject. "What are we going to do about the ants?"

"We can set the chickens on them!" Janie's dad told her. "And the chickens will eat them all up as quick as a wink!"

"And how quick is a wink?" Janie asked. "I don't much like those ants crawling around all over the place."

"We could try some horse fly spray on them," Janie's mother offered as she turned the eggs over in the skillet, and then lifted them out two at a time placing the eggs on the plates already set on the table.

"I wanted my eggs scrambled," Janie told her, to which Janie's mother simply shook her head.

"When I asked you two how you wanted your eggs cooked, I only got *one* somewhat convoluted answer, and that was from your dad," Janie's mother told her. "So, now I'm afraid you are stuck with what I cooked!"

"But we have *plenty* of eggs!" Janie protested.

The Horses of Griffin Farm

"Waste not, want not!" Janie's dad told her. "I suggest you eat those eggs," he added, as four slices of toast popped up from the toaster, and as Janie's mom brought the toast to the table and set out some butter and raspberry jam.

"Is that the jam we made from the wild raspberries we gathered in the forest?" Janie asked.

"Sure is!" Janie's mother replied, as she sat down at her place at the table.

"Yummy!" Janie exclaimed. "Yummy!" she repeated.

"I have some very nice apples for the horses," Janie's mother announced.

"And an apple a day keeps the doctor away!" Janie's father exclaimed.

Janie's mother shook her head.

"Actually, apples have quite a bit of sugar in them; and if you eat too much sugar that isn't good for you, and it could lead to type two diabetes and tooth decay."

And now, it was Janie's dad's turn to shake his head.

"Everything in moderation!" he added.

Janie smiled. She thought everything, including this repartee at the breakfast table, was fun; and so, she had something to add as well.

"I've been thinking a lot about ants," she began.

"I could tell you'd been thinking about *something*, and thinking is good," her father interrupted her with a smile. "So, tell us what you have been thinking about ants."

"Well, I have been thinking about how organized ants are and how well the ants work together for the common good of all of the other ants."

"Much better than people," her father interrupted again.

"Yes," Janie replied, affirming what her father had just said, as Janie's mom just ate her eggs and toast. "And what I have been thinking, or rather wondering, is whether we are just somebody's ants, going through life on the top of an orange or something."

"Well, we could be," Janie's dad told her. "I mean there are many mysteries in life, and this could possibly be one of them."

"Then maybe we shouldn't kill ants at all," Janie said, after thinking for just a moment.

"Well, all creatures great and small do have their place on this earth," Janie's dad said, as her mother continued to say nothing.

"What do *you* think, Mother?" Janie's dad asked Janie's mother.

"I think you two better eat your eggs and toast before they get cold," Janie's mother told the two of them.

And so, nothing more was said; and they all ate their eggs and toast before their eggs and toast became so cold only the ants would eat them. And, of course, they also drank some orange juice; and

The Horses of Griffin Farm

Janie's mom and dad had their coffee. (And everything they ate and drank was organic, of course, even the eggs; because the chickens were fed organic chicken feed!)

However, Janie was still not sure she liked having ants around everywhere, even though she admired their work ethic as well as their purpose, and even though she wondered if people were all just a bunch of ants on top of a greater being's orange.

CHAPTER FOUR

EXACTLY WHAT IS A GRIFFIN?

The griffin is an ancient creature arising from fairytales, myths and legends. It has the body, tail, and back legs of a lion; and as fables tell us, it also has the head and the wings of the majestic eagle, and the talons of the eagle at its front. And, just in case you are wondering how this mythological creature came to be, I can tell you the answer is quite simple. It's because the lion has always been considered the king of the jungle, and the eagle has always been considered the king of the birds! And all down through the ages of mankind, the griffin has been revered in myth and tradition as the most powerful, as well as the most majestic creature of all creatures, a creature that would guard the priceless treasures of man, especially man's hidden treasures of gold!

Now, while Griffin Farm did not have any gold or priceless treasure, Griffin Farm had a treasure all of its own. And since the sign on the entrance to Griffin Farm, bore the graphic symbol of the Griffin, it was a warning to all who entered its twenty-six acres bordered by forest that extended for miles, that Griffin Farm was guarded by and had the protection of the griffin.

And the treasure it guarded might not have been immediately noticed by others, but the treasure it guarded was much more precious than silver or gold. The treasure it guarded was the treasure of promise and of love. However, there was never really any real discussion on the subject amongst the family. There was only the giving and the caring and the sharing of love.

And this was how all of the days at Griffin Farm proceeded. There was a caring, a love and a sharing, not only for one another, but also for the creatures that lived there, even if the ants were of dubious value to Janie.

And so, each day proceeded much as the previous day. There were chores to do. Horses were put out to pasture. Horses were ridden and exercised on a somewhat revolving schedule. There were riding lessons for Janie, and more. No one ever said they had nothing to do on Griffin Farm, and no one ever said they were bored on Griffin Farm; because even if you came for a visit, you were naturally drawn into everything going on right *there* on Griffin Farm, and that included the chores that had to be done, as well as all of the love, the caring and the sharing, and all of the fun to be had on Griffin Farm.

The work was long. The work was very tiring. The treasure was priceless. But there was even more to the treasure.

The Horses of Griffin Farm

This was about rescuing horses, and so that afternoon as the family of three met at the kitchen table for lunch, the discussion continued.

"Do you really think we have a treasure to protect, and is that why we call this place Griffin Farm?" Janie asked.

"Yes, but you already know that," Janie's mother told her. "I told you all about the griffins."

"Do you think the griffins were ever real, like the dinosaurs?" Janie asked.

"Maybe the dinosaurs weren't even real," Janie's dad joked. "Everything is how you perceive it," he added.

"But we've seen dinosaur bones in the natural history museum, so they *have* to be real!" Janie protested.

"Oh really?" Janie's dad questioned. "Maybe those bones are just fakes."

"And maybe man never landed on the moon," Janie's mother added. "Maybe everything is just fake. Maybe everything we think is real is merely a fragment of the imagination of another being greater than man, putting thoughts and ideas into our mortal heads."

Janie shook her head feigning disbelief and smiled, knowing her parents weren't *really* serious about what they were saying.

"Well, I *do* feel real," she said, wide-eyed, playing into the game of thought her parents were playing with her.

"Of course, you do," her dad told her. "That's all a part of it."

And then, Janie wanted the teasing to stop; and so, she decided to just let go of what her parents were saying, hoping they would simply stop the teasing.

"All that I really know is that I love you both," Janie told her parents. "And I love the horses too, and all the other animals on the farm. And I don't care if anything is really real, because it all feels real to me . . . especially all of the love and the caring and the sharing in this house!"

"And *that* is our treasure," Janie's father told her. "The love and the caring and the sharing are our treasure, and the griffin will protect that!"

And then . . . all was said that needed to be said; and so, nothing more was said.

And the day continued . . . as all days must.

CHAPTER FIVE

HORSES FOR THE RICH

There is something about horses few know. And that is that just like people, horses can develop ulcers. And in horses this is simply called the 'gastric ulcer syndrome'. Gastric ulcers, also known as stomach ulcers, are terrible sores that form in the stomach lining of a horse. And unbeknownst to most of us, they are quite common in horses. While ulcers may affect any horse, and at any age, they most often occur in athletic horses, horses that engage in endurance events, horse shows and racing. And the reason for this is exercise simply increases gastric acid production and decreases blood flow to the horse's intestinal tract. And when the horse exercises, the stomach's acidic fluid splashes all over inside the stomach lining of the horse, and exposes the upper and much more vulnerable portion of the stomach to a very acidic ph.

And this means that to the very rich, the horse loses value; because it cannot perform as the wealthy require. You see, to have a

The Horses of Griffin Farm

horse that performs well is one thing; but to have a horse that cannot perform or cannot earn money winning races (if the horse is a racehorse) is quite another thing altogether.

And because racehorses are younger horses, it is the younger horse who often ends up being sent to slaughter due to a simple gastric ulcer. However, this was not the only reason the rich sent horses to slaughter.

And this is why Janie and her family ended up in the business of rescuing horses. You see, it was one thing to set a horse out to pasture after it had lived a full and long life, but it was quite another thing (especially to Janie and her family) to take a horse, any horse, to slaughter, especially when that horse could be saved and become sound.

And besides, Janie dearly loved her horses, all of them. And while the family could ill afford to feed and house every horse they rescued from slaughter, they could afford to nurse them back to health and either sell them or rent them out as lesson horses. At least that was the plan.

And so, Janie and her mom and dad went to horse auctions and made bids on some of the younger horses doomed to slaughter for one reason or another. And even though they couldn't afford to bring them all home, all at once, they could (and did) manage to save a few horses, one at a time, the horses that became famously known as 'the horses of Griffin Farm'.

The Horses of Griffin Farm

And those horses all took home in one of the two barns on the Griffin Farm property, barns which Janie's mother conceded were sound, and in some respects in better repair than the old farmhouse that had been long standing on the property when they purchased Griffin Farm.

And each horse they brought onto the property of Griffin Farm was seen by a vet, given love and encouragement, and properly fed and cared for . . . in the hope that each rescue would result in a healthy and sound animal.

And so, this was not only the beginning of Griffin Farm, it was also the beginning of a great family adventure. And no one in Janie's family of three had any idea where the adventure would lead them.

And the exploitive rich had no idea what damage they were doing to these majestic animals, and no real idea or inclination toward saving them, as they thought only about their own instantaneous gratification. But as the saying goes, "One person's trash is another person's treasure.' And this is also why the sign on the front gate of the property read, 'Griffin Farm'. You see, what the griffin was protecting, *was* truly a treasure! And, after all, love does cure and conquer all manner of evil.

The Horses of Griffin Farm

CHAPTER SIX

THE DOGS OF GRIFFIN FARM

As Janie set about brushing down the horses, cleaning their hooves and tending to their feed, her father entered the barn where she was tending to her chores. He was followed by one of their seven dogs.

Janie looked up for a moment and asked, "Why do we have so many dogs, Dad?"

"Well, we won't keep them all. The puppies are in training,"

"In training?" Janie asked.

"Yes," Janie's father told her. "But they're only *sort of* in training."

"But why are the puppies only *sort of* in training? They're all pretty big already. I don't understand," Janie told her father.

"Well, it's because they aren't exactly 'in training'. We're just sort of civilizing them, so to speak, so that means they are 'only sort of in training'. You see, we have Anatolian Shepherd Dogs, which are

The Horses of Griffin Farm

a very independent type of dog breed. Historically, in ancient times, they (quite often) literally had to find their own food; and they survived by hunting gophers and other small animals. Their instinct was (and still is) basically to take care of themselves and the flock without needing any actual instruction. But it seems your mother feels we should at least civilize them. And they certainly don't have to hunt for food here on the farm. Our dog food bill will attest to that!" Janie's father said with a grin.

And then Janie asked, "But why are our dogs so much bigger than the dogs on the other farms, anyway? It's like they're monsters or something."

"Oh, they're *not* monsters," Janie's father told her. "In fact, quite to the contrary, they are exactly the opposite of being monsters. They're the guardians of the flocks! And that's why we are breeding them, and that's why the neighboring farms all want a puppy. And as to their large size . . . simple genetics have determined the size of this breed."

"I don't understand," Janie told her father.

"Then, I will explain it to you," her father said, as he picked up one of the brushes in a metal tack box sitting on a low wooden bench and began to brush down the horse alongside his daughter. "The kind of dogs we have, Anatolian Shepherd Dogs, as I have told you, are bred to guard and protect livestock. It's believed that this particular breed of dog originated in Turkey, where they are still used today for exactly that purpose. And our dogs will protect us, and our property, and all our other animals from predators."

"Is that why they're so big?" Janie asked.

"I would guess so," Janie's father told her; and then he added, "You see, our dogs are an incredibly old and ancient breed of dog. And survival of all creatures is based on natural selection, or in how they are bred by their owners. Since the larger dogs were preferred as the guardians of the flocks when the dogs were bred, the largest of these dogs were more than likely chosen to be bred to one another. And even more interesting is that an artifact has been found dating all the way back to 2000 B.C. describing a dog in the Anatolian region of Turkey that fits the exact description of the Anatolian Shepherd Dogs that we have today, large and strong with a heavy head! Even the Bible talks about them in the Old Testament in 'The Book of Job' (also set in Turkey); and it dates these dogs all the way back to 1800 B.C.! *And it actually describes these very same, very large dogs living amongst the flocks and the people of 1800 B.C.!*"

"I think that's more than I really wanted to know," Janie said, somewhat flippantly, just as her mother entered the barn, and as Janie continued (right along with her father) brushing down the horse before them.

"You'd better watch your mouth," her mother told her, knowing Janie's father was heavy on detail and somewhat precise when it came to answering *any* question; but not offering any leeway to Janie of any sort.

"Sorry," Janie told her father.

"But did you tell her the *real* reason this breed of dog is so important in the world right now?" Janie's mother asked Janie's father.

"Not exactly," came the reply.

"I take that to mean 'not at all'," Janie's mother said, who was a stickler for preciseness and for saying what you mean and meaning what you say.

And then she went into her diatribe.

"Anatolian Shepherds," she began, "didn't gain popularity here in America until the Endangered Species Act was passed in 1973. Then those charged with enforcing the act began to look at how to control livestock predators, that were now protected species as defined under the act. In the past, these predators (that were now endangered species) were simply hunted down and killed. And now, this was no longer allowed under the Endangered Species Act."

"So, what did they do about the predators?" Janie asked.

"They did a very good thing," her mother told her. "The solution was simple! Use livestock guardian dogs that could easily deter predators from attacking flocks simply by being present."

"Do you mean like our dogs?" Janie asked.

The Horses of Griffin Farm

"Yes," her mother told her. "You see, all creatures great and small have a purpose, and it is better to be chased away in a natural fashion than to be killed by a trap or a bullet."

Janie smiled. Everything she had been told made a lot of sense now to our young Janie. And she loved her life on Griffin Farm.

CHAPTER SEVEN
THE CAT AND THE MOUSE

Janie's family had house cats and outdoor cats, because they used to live in a house next to a canyon before they'd moved to Griffin Farm. And the canyon was rife with rats that would ever so boldly enter the house.

The logical way to get rid of the rats coming into the house was, of course to have cats take care of them, and Janie's mom knew that because she had grown up in the country where her mom and dad raised and ate organic food, and where absolutely everything was done naturally and without the use of poisons. Janie's mother's mom and dad would even go so far as to trap unwanted rats, gophers and other animals and take them to a nearby sanctuary to be freed. And what they couldn't trap, they had cats (and lots of them) to take up the slack. Some of them were feral cats who simply appeared on the scene, and some were pets that lived mostly indoors, meaning they came in at night or when called to sleep or to eat. At one point, Janie's grandmother counted seventeen cats on the property; and once, when Janie's grandmother opened the door to go outside, all seventeen cats jumped from the house roof to the ground, supposedly looking for something to eat.

"It's raining cats!" Janie's mother exclaimed that day; and it was a story Janie's grandmother often liked to tell.

It wasn't that Janie's grandparents liked to collect cats, or anything like that, it was just that the cats seemed to appear out of nowhere; and because they were useful, they were fed.

And this is why Janie's mother came to certain conclusions about cats, and why they not only had indoor cats, they had outdoor cats as well. In fact, they had a certain barn cat that took care of the birds and mice in their barns, as well as in their garage. He would catch the unwanted creatures the dogs failed to chase away and leave them for Janie's mother in front of the front door and the back door of the farmhouse where Janie's mother could find them.

One day Janie saw a mouse scurrying about inside the tack room which was always kept closed.

Janie (for some unknown reason) became frightened; and so, she ran straightaway to her mother.

"There's a mouse in the tack room!" Janie shouted as she ran toward the house. "There's a mouse in the tack room!" Janie shouted once again as she neared where her mother was standing outside the back door contemplating the coming weather.

The Horses of Griffin Farm

Janie's mother laughed.

"Well," she said, as she and Janie headed for the tack room. "I believe I know exactly what to do about that!"

Janie smiled. Her mother was very smart and always seemed to know what to do, just as mothers were always supposed to know what to do.

So, when they arrived at the tack room, the solution was simple! Janie's mother simply went into the tack room and called out to the cat.

"Pinky! Pinky!" Janie's mother called out.

And before they knew it, Pinky the cat came running towards them.

"There's a mouse inside the tack room!" Janie's mother told the cat. "Go and get it!"

And so, as they left the tack room (with the door now open) and headed out to groom the horses, Pinky the cat did exactly as she was told.

And then, all was right with the world, at least for the time being; and nature took its course and did exactly what nature was supposed to do . . . all thanks to Pinky the cat!

You see, on the farm everyone had work to do, and that included Pinky the cat!

CHAPTER EIGHT
THE HORSES OF THE HOUSE

Janie's family had horses, six to be exact, and one large pony, not to mention all the chickens, pigs, ducks, and geese, all of which needed to be fed and cared for on a daily basis.

"We live in a zoo!" Janie's mother exclaimed, as she hefted a flake of hay into one of the eating troughs of one of the horses.

The horses they had were members of their family, and although they had rescued them from auction, or perhaps *because* they had rescued them from auction, they each had their places in the house, so to speak, even if they lived in the barns; because in the house, the talk was often (and more than likely) all about the horses! And (if truth be told) Janie would have simply loved it if the horses could either move inside the house, or if she could simply move into one of their two barns.

"Did you know that in Denmark the horses and the other animals lived in rooms in basements right under peoples houses, or in

The Horses of Griffin Farm

rooms right next to people's houses, when your great, great grandfather was a boy?" Janie's mother asked Janie, as Janie entered the barn to help her mother with the watering and the feeding of the horses, and (of course) to feed and water the one large pony they had that was patiently waiting to be fed and watered.

"That is so cool!" Janie told her.

"The Danish people did that to keep their houses warm," Janie's mother continued.

"And I guess that also meant no one had to go outside during the cold Danish winters to feed them!" Janie replied.

Janie's mother laughed.

"But how did keeping horses in the basement, or in a room next to the house, keep anyone warm?" Janie asked.

"The body heat and the excrement of the animals created a warmth that either rose up into the house from what we think of as a basement of the house, or it came into the house from the room built for them next to the house," Janie's mother further explained.

"That must have smelled pretty awful," Janie said, wrinkling her nose.

"They probably just got used to the smell and didn't notice it," Janie's mother replied, as she lifted a flake of hay from the bale she'd brought into the barn and placed it in the trough of yet another horse.

"I wouldn't mind sleeping in the barn," Janie said. "And I don't think the horses would mind sleeping in the house with us, or under it, or in a room next to the house. It sounds like a good idea to me."

"Well, apparently your great, great grandfather wasn't as appreciative of the idea as you seem to be, Janie."

"Why do you say that, Mom?"

"Well, he left home when he was only sixteen, Janie. And he joined a tramp steamer as a cabin boy and went off to see the world!"

"You never told me that before," Janie said, wrinkling her forehead. "How could he have ever left the farm? Farms are so cool."

"I guess he didn't like living in a zoo," Janie's mother told her, to which Janie began to laugh.

"But it's so much fun!" Janie protested.

"It's also a lot of work, Janie. And maybe your great, great grandfather wanted more out of life."

"Did he find what he wanted after he left home?" Janie asked.

"I believe so, Janie," Janie's mother told her, as she went to the bale of hay for another flake of hay.

"He did just about everything you could ever imagine," Janie's mother told her. "He was even a gaucho in Argentina!"

"What was his name?" Janie asked.

"His name was Julius Petersen," her mother told her. "And his travels took him to meet a lot of very famous people."

"I'm supposed to write an essay for school about someone in my family tree. Do you think I could write an essay about him?"

"I don't see why not," Janie's mother replied. "He was an interesting person. And he was so smart."

"But didn't he leave school?" Janie asked.

"There are other ways to be smart, and in those days not everyone had the privilege of going to school like you do."

Janie thought for a moment, wrinkling her forehead again.

"Don't do that too much," her mother told her. "Your face could get stuck that way."

"I was just thinking, Mom," Janie said.

"Now, don't get any ideas about heading off into the sunset. You have work to do right here and right now. And besides, times are changing. Things aren't at all like what they once were."

"What do you mean by that?" Janie asked.

"Just think about it, and you will figure it out," Janie's mother told her. "Now, get to work!" she added. "I can use the help!"

And so, Janie set about helping her mother with the feeding and the watering of the horses; and as she did that, she thought about what her mother had said.

And finally, as the last of the horses in the two barns were fed and watered, she asked, "Can you tell me some more about my great, great grandfather, Julius Petersen?"

And her mother replied, "Of course!"

CHAPTER NINE
UNDER THE OLD MAPLE TREE

Janie and her mother walked to the bench beneath the old maple tree situated between the two horse barns and sat down amongst the budding tulips. It was spring; and soon (before either of them knew it) it would be summer. But now it was time to enjoy the fresh air of spring before the mosquitoes and the other unwelcome insects arrived.

"I just love spring," Janie's mother told her, as the two of them sat down on the somewhat weathered wooden bench beneath the old maple tree. "Do you hear the birds singing?" she asked, as Janie nodded her head in affirmation of the question. "The birds remind me of the day your great, great grandfather died."

"Do you mean Julius Peterson?" Janie asked. "You did say that was his name."

"Yes, Janie. That is who I mean. And he was a great man, and he was kind and loving."

"He was a great man?" Janie asked, choosing what she wanted to hear next

"Yes, Janie. He was a great man. And he saw and he did *a lot* during his time on this earth."

Janie leaned toward her mother, listening intently now to what her mother had to say.

"Did you know he was an inventor?" Janie's mother asked.

"No, I didn't. No one ever told me much about him at all," Janie replied.

"Well, then . . . I will tell you what I know from the beginning," Janie's mother continued. "After Julius left home and hopped abroad the tramp steamer boat, he worked hard, first as a cabin boy, and then as a deck hand. He shoveled coal at one point to stoke the boat's furnace. And even though he began to cough, he kept on working. Finally, the boat reached Argentina; and he was coughing so much that the ship's captain insisted he go and see a doctor."

"Oh my," Janie interrupted her mother momentarily. "How sick was he?"

"The visit with the doctor ended up with him hearing some awfully bad news. He was diagnosed with tuberculosis, a disease that could have killed him."

"Killed him?" Janie asked.

"Yes," Janie's mother continued.

"Well, then what happened?" Janie asked, imploring her mother to continue.

"The doctor told him to not return to the boat. He told him he needed to get some fresh air and relax."

Janie was full of wonder.

"So, did he relax?" she asked.

"Not exactly, Janie," came the reply. "He became an Argentinean gaucho."

And now, Janie had even more questions.

"So, what is a gaucho?" Janie asked, wide-eyed.

"A gaucho is a cowboy of the South American pampas," Janie's mother explained.

"Do you mean that my great, great grandfather was a South American cowboy? Janie asked, quite impressed by the idea of it all.

"Yes," Janie's mother told her. "And so, I guess the apple doesn't fall so very far from the proverbial apple tree," she added, as she placed her hand lovingly upon Janie's shoulder.

"Tell me more about these gauchos," Janie pleaded.

"The gauchos are legendary South American folk heroes, famed for their hardiness and lawlessness . . . although I don't believe your great, great grandfather was at all lawless," Janie's mother paused, and then continued. "Your great, great grandfather rounded up herds of horses and cattle that roamed freely on the grasslands of

The Horses of Griffin Farm

Argentina, just like those gauchos that came before him, except perhaps with less flair than those gauchos of the eighteenth and nineteenth centuries. But that is yet *another* story for yet *another* time. Let's just say that being a gaucho in Argentina was still a very romantic thing to be in your great, great grandfather's time! In fact, it is a fact that Argentine writers have celebrated the gauchos of South America over time immemorial; and gaucho literature and the gaucho history over time immemorial is an important part of the Argentine cultural tradition."

"But how and why did he come to America?" Janie asked. "It seems like he was living a dream come true."

"Dreams grow, and dreams sometimes change. And your great, great grandfather was a young man living in his own adventurous dream. And how and why he came to America happens to be another important part of his very own story," Janie's mother told her. "And that is the part of the story I will tell you next. Because there is (indeed) a lot more to tell of this story!"

And so, the story continued.

CHAPTER TEN
Continuing The Story

"Your great, great, Grandpa Petersen, made a deal with a fellow gaucho from Germany," Janie's mother continued.

"A deal?" Janie asked. "What kind of a deal did he make?"

"Well, the German, whose last name was Meyer, noticed your great, great grandfather was quite clever in the way he did things. He noticed that your great, great grandfather was mechanical and methodical in the way he did things. And the German wasn't so inclined, but he had money to invest. And your great, great grandfather had already invented a device for hitching boats to tow boats with another individual, and *that* was actually patented in the United States by his partner in that endeavor."

"Did he make any money off of that patent?" Janie asked.

"No. I don't think so," her mother told her. "Nothing was ever about making money with your great, great grandfather. The thing for him was in the invention."

The Horses of Griffin Farm

"I don't understand."

"Well, it was the age of invention back then; and great strides were being made in the inventing of things and in the inventing of the way of doing things. And it was all extremely exciting for a young man like your great, great grandfather."

"So, what happened with the German man?" Janie asked.

"Well, after a period of time, the length of which I am not certain, one night as a group of the gauchos sat warming themselves by a campfire, a discussion began between the men about this time of invention, and (of course) your great, great grandfather was deep in the thick of things. And then, later as the group broke up and headed for their tents for the night, your great, great grandfather and the German decided to make a deal whereas your great, great grandfather would travel ahead to America and sharpen his skills in the emerging field of electricity in the hope that it would eventually lead to the two of them forming an electrical company."

"And did that ever happen?" Janie asked, her face skewed in inquisitive expression.

"No. It didn't. Your great, great grandfather did *leave* Argentina, hopping aboard another steam trammer not long thereafter," Janie's mother explained. "But the business between your great, great grandfather and the German never got off the ground."

"But why not?" Janie asked.

The Horses of Griffin Farm

"It seems the German got thrown from his horse in some sort of cattle stampede and was found unconscious. Sadly, he ended up dying of his injuries," Janie's mother told her, as she lowered her eyes. "At least that is the message received by your great, great grandfather some years later."

"So, what happened next?"

"Julius Petersen was never one to give up on anything; and so, he moved ahead with his dreams, just as you should do. He got a job with the General Electric Company, and he was instrumental in the invention and was listed (as an inventor) on several patents held by the General Electric Company," Janie's mother told her.

"Like what?" Janie asked, as she was full of questions.

"Well, he was the inventor of the sealed beam headlight first used by Henry Ford at the Ford Company of its time. And it is still used today!"

"So, did my great, great grandfather become rich?"

"No. It seems that even though he invented the sealed beam headlight, because he was in the employment of the General Electric Company, he got nothing extra for his efforts because under contract the General Electric Company owned all rights to anything produced, created or invented by its employees according to the terms of the employment contract," Janie's mother explained. "And this is still how companies conduct business today."

"But that doesn't seem fair!" Janie protested.

"No. It isn't. But your grandfather didn't really care. You see the thrill was in the invention, and the idea that he could invent something that was useful and went on through time was what kept him going on to inventing new things. He invented things for the joy of the act of inventing, not to get rich or to make money. And this went on through the days of the world's great depression."

"He must have been amazing," Janie interjected into the ongoing conversation.

"Oh, he was!" Janie's mother exclaimed with pride. "He even knew the Wright Brothers and Henry Ford and Thomas Alva Edison!"

"Wow! That is amazing!" Janie interjected, again wide-eyed.

"And he invented a device that measures the weight of water for the bathyscape at Scripps Institute of Oceanography, which led to a lot of ocean exploration at great depths of the ocean; and when he died, way back in the 1970's, he was working on the invention of an air combustion engine that would have eliminated the need for oil and gas to run the motors of cars. If he had lived, we might not have had the global warming crisis we have now."

"What happened to those plans?" Janie asked.

"His family laughed at him. And when he died, the plans disappeared. I don't know what happened to the plans. They were never sent to the patent office," Janie's mother told her.

"You mean my great, great grandfather could have saved the world? He could have saved the world from global warming and could have saved millions and millions of people lost as a result of global warming?" Janie asked, incredulously.

"That was what he wanted," Janie's mother explained. "He was never about money. You see, inventing for a greater purpose was his dream."

"I get that," Janie said. "But I don't get why his family didn't continue on with the invention."

"The only one who was interested in doing that was your grandfather, and they just laughed at him for believing in your great, great grandfather; and they presumedly destroyed the plans along with the working air combustion engine and just got rid of it and sold it as scrap. And so, the dream died."

"Do you mean that had my great, great grandfather lived everyone would be driving in cars and trucks powered by air combustion engines?" Janie asked rhetorically, shaking her head in disbelief.

"That's exactly what I mean; and he died in my father's arms beneath an orchard tree where he had been helping to dig a watering ring around the tree. And your aunt and I were very young; and as he died, we gathered flowers to place in his lap, and my mother (your grandmother) ran to call 911. But it didn't help."

"Did he say anything before he died?" Janie asked.

"He only said, 'I feel funny,' and then . . . he was gone; and just the night before *that,* he was telling your dad all about his air combustion engine and his working model, and how the other family members laughed at him."

"Did your dad (my grandpa) laugh at him?" Janie asked, somewhat redundantly, because her mother had just told her how her grandfather had believed in his grandfather and the invention.

"Not at all. He was intrigued. Your great, great grandfather had invented many things during his time, and he was a great man. And as for me, I was only three years old at the time; and I was angry at God, so angry that I refused to pray after they took him away. And so, my mother (your grandmother) called the pastor of the church to come and talk with me; and he brought with him the empty shell of a tortoise from the Bahamas (where he had previously been a pastor) and he told me that when they took my grandpa away (because I believed he was my grandpa, not my great grandpa) that all they took was a shell, and that just like the turtle, and just like the part that was the turtle was gone from the shell, my grandpa was just gone from his shell until the time we met again in heaven."

"And did you believe him?" Janie asked, again wide-eyed and listening intently.

"Yes. I believed him. And this is why I followed all my dreams in this life and why you should follow all your dreams in *your* life."

"You mean, before we leave our shells?" Janie asked.

"Exactly," Janie's mother told her, as tears welled in her eyes. "You see, we only have this life here and now to make our here and now dreams come true."

And Janie knew and understood exactly what her mother was saying. And she knew her life would have a purpose just like her great, great grandfather's life had a purpose. And she also knew that purpose had nothing to do with money. It only had to do with her dreams for other living things and for herself, and she knew that just like her great, great grandfather, even if others laughed at her for those dreams, she would (indeed) make certain all her dreams would come true. And she also knew that she would never, ever give up on her dreams and that she would work hard to make her dreams come true up to her dying day.

CHAPTER ELEVEN
ABOUT THE HORSE AUCTIONS

"There's a horse auction this weekend," Janie's mother announced one summer morning, as Janie and her father sat down at the breakfast table after having fed and watered the horses and other animals. "I think we should go to it."

"I agree!" Janie's father exclaimed. "It will be fun!"

"Why are horses even sent to auction?" Janie asked her mother and father, sincerely desirous of knowing the answer, which was for now ignored, perhaps even unheard, as Janie's mother put the scrambled eggs she had been cooking on the stove on a large plate and set it on the table.

"I can scramble more eggs," Janie's mother said. "So please don't be shy about taking your share," she added, as she turned to take the freshly browned toast from the toaster.

"I just love scrambled eggs and toast with butter and our wild raspberry jam," Janie said, as she piled her plate high with scrambled eggs and reached for the plate of toast to remove a slice of toast to add to her plate.

"Well," Janie's father said, "I guess that makes gathering all those wild raspberries and cooking over that hot stove to make those jars of homemade raspberry jam worth it!"

"It sure does!" Janie told her father, as she finished buttering her toast and reached for the jar of jam. "It's so yummy!" she added enthusiastically with a smile from ear to ear.

"I do love your enthusiasm," Janie's mother said, as she took her place at the table.

"Will you be coming to the horse auction with us this weekend, as you usually do?" Janie's mother asked, fearing Janie may have already made other plans for the weekend with her friends. "Your dad and I sure could use your keen eye for horses to decide on which horses we should bid. And we thought maybe we would find that special horse for you!"

Janie smiled.

"Of course, I'm going!" Janie exclaimed excitedly. "But I'm still wondering about something," Janie said, returning somewhat to her earlier as yet unanswered question.

"And what would that be?" Janie's father asked.

"I was wondering why people got rid of their horses in the first place and why do they get rid of them at auction. I mean, why are they even sent to an auction? Don't people care about what happens to their horses?" Janie asked, in her sweetly naive way.

"Well," Janie's father began, "It is incredibly sad. However, auctions do provide the only public place where people who conduct these kinds of sales can check out a horses' condition prior to putting them up for sale at auction. The sad part is auctions indirectly actually promote the neglect of horses, because auctions provide a legal manner of sale for both abused as well as neglected horses. And, in fact, if there were no auctions, irresponsible horse owners and unscrupulous dealers would have no place to sell their horses."

I don't understand that at all," Janie told her father. "It doesn't seem at all fair."

"The truth is we go to these horse auctions to rescue horses," Janie's mother explained. "A lot of people don't really love their horses, like we love our horses. Some people buy and sell horses merely for profit. And if a horse doesn't perform as an unscrupulous owner expects it to perform, the horse becomes a liability to the unscrupulous owner. And that's because it's expensive to feed and to care for horses, because horses are such large animals."

"But why don't they grow their own hay and send the horses out to pasture for their food?" Janie asked.

"For some people, a horse is a status symbol. For others, a horse is an animal they can race and bet on; and when the horse doesn't win or even perform as the often-wealthy owner expects, the horse

The Horses of Griffin Farm

becomes a liability. It doesn't pay its own way in life, so it is sent to auction; and sometimes even young horses are bought up at action for slaughter," Janie's father interjected as Janie sat wide-eyed, fork in hand, not at all eating the bit of scrambled eggs tottering atop her fork.

"But why slaughter?" Janie asked. "They don't use horses for glue anymore here, because glue is synthetic now; and they don't use horses for dog food anymore either."

"That's true. But some foreign countries don't prohibit such things; and so, horses (sadly) still have value for those uses," Janie's father told her. "In some countries horses are even butchered for meat people eat!"

"And so, is this why we go to auction to save horses?" Janie asked.

"Yes. It is," Janie's mother interjected. "But it is also because we love horses, and I just can't stand to see such noble creatures being abused and being sent to early deaths."

"Then I'm very lucky," Janie told her parents with a smile. "Because I have the very, very best parents in the whole wide world! And I just love all of our horses!"

Janie's parents smiled at her and lovingly nodded their heads.

And then, Janie's mother told Janie and her father to eat their scrambled eggs and toast before the breakfast became cold, and so they did just that . . . after which, Janie headed outside to complete the remaining chores of the day, including exercising the horses.

CHAPTER TWELVE
ON THE WAY TO THE AUCTION

"I was thinking," Janie began, and then paused for a moment, as they headed out to the horse auction on that Saturday, towing their horse trailer behind the family's dual cabbed truck.

"It's nice to know you've been thinking," Janie's father quipped. "Thinking is a good thing, I think."

Janie was used to her father making light of things, and so she just ignored him and continued on expressing her thoughts.

"Well, I was thinking that it must be sad for a horse to be hauled away from its home. If I was a horse, I wouldn't like that."

"Then it's a good thing you're not a horse," her father told her, as he continued to drive down the road, nearing the auction. "And it's a good thing you're a kidlet!"

Janie laughed, as her mother shook her head.

"It's sad because horses are herd animals," her mother explained, "and when a horse is removed from the herd, it not only

The Horses of Griffin Farm

effects the horse that's being removed, it also affects the remaining horses. The herd is the horse's family. It's just like we are a family; and if you take one of us away, all of us will be hurt."

"Do you think our horses think we are a part of their herd?" Janie asked her mother from the back seat of the dual cabbed truck.

"I do. I really do," Janie's mother told her, as Janie's dad whinnied like a horse from the driver's seat of the truck, and they all burst into laughter.

"I'm so excited about getting this horse!" Janie suddenly blurted out from the backseat of the dual cabbed truck.

"We must choose carefully, Obi-Wan Kenobi," her father replied, ever so mockingly, even though what he was saying was actually true.

"Will we have to quarantine the horse again from the other horses when we bring it home?" Janie asked, as their truck and trailer pulled into the large dirt parking lot at the auction, having at last arrived.

"Of course!" her mother told her.

"But why?" Janie asked. "Why do we always have to do that?"

"Well," Janie's mother began. "It's because people who bring their horses to auction aren't always honest. Some of them don't bother to properly vaccinate their horses, and sometimes a horse could be sick. And we don't want to make our other horses sick when the new horse joins its new herd."

The Horses of Griffin Farm

"But I thought people had to show proof of vaccinations when they brought their horses to the auction," Janie protested. "So why do we always need to quarantine the horses we get at a horse auction?"

"It's because some people aren't honest," Janie's father interjected. "They make up fake vaccination papers."

"But that's terrible!" Janie said. "Why do they do that?"

"There are a lot of bad people in this world doing a lot of terrible things," Janie's father told her, as their vehicle and attached horse trailer pulled to a halting stop.

"I don't think I like bad people," Janie told her father. "I don't like bad people at all," she added.

"Sometimes good people do terrible things for what they think is the right reason," Janie's mother said, as the three of them unfastened their seatbelts. "But horses aren't like people."

Janie thought for a moment and then she asked, "Well, since the horse has to be quarantined, can I camp out with it while it's being quarantined?"

"You've never done that before," Janie's mother told her. "So why now?"

"I don't know," Janie told her mother. "This time I just have a feeling about it. That's all. I just think I need to do this."

"We must keep the kidlet happy!" Janie's father said, as he turned and smiled at Janie's mother. "And the weather is good. So why not?" he asked; and Janie's mother agreed.

CHAPTER THIRTEEN
THE CHOOSING

Janie and her mother and father walked toward the auction area passing the pens where the auction horses were stabled. And while they weren't allowed to stop and inspect any of the horses as they made their way toward the bleachers in the auction area, Janie (even at her tender age) had an idea about what she wanted in any horse they would acquire.

"This time you get to choose the horse we bid on," Janie's father told her. "We told you we thought maybe we would find that special horse for you; and your mother and I agreed this should be your choice and your horse," Janie's father added, hoping the family bankbook would cover the choice.

Janie smiled.

"I'd like a horse with kind eyes," Janie told her father, as she made note in her head of each horse she passed . . . prodded by her parents to please not dawdle.

The Horses of Griffin Farm

"I'd like you to have an animal with a good constitution and four strong legs,' Janie's father scoffed. "But this is your choice, Janie."

"A young horse would be nice," Janie's mother interjected, as they at last reached the auction area and took their seats mid-bleacher. And then she added as a side thought, "I had the best horse in the whole wide world when I was a kid your age! She was green broke and only two years old when I got her. The owners wanted more than your grandparents could afford, so we bargained for her."

"Her?" Janie asked. "She was a mare?"

"Yes," Janie's mother told her. "And she really was the best horse in the whole wide world! Her name was Sassafras! And I called her Sassy!"

"Why did you call her that?" Janie asked with furrowed brow.

"I called her that because she was sassy, just like I was!" Janie's mother told her with a laugh. "And my parents (your grandparents) couldn't have agreed more. They took one look at that green broke horse and decided that Sassy was the horse for me!"

"But I thought you said they couldn't afford the horse."

"They couldn't. But the woman who was selling it wanted it to have a good and loving home. And so, she said she was willing to bargain," Janie's mother explained.

"And so, what was the final price?" Janie asked.

Janie's mother smiled.

49

The Horses of Griffin Farm

"Well, she wanted a lot more, but your grandparents offered her five hundred dollars; and I threw in the bicycle I had just won at a talent contest for doing my tap-dancing routine. And that sealed the deal!"

"You were a tap dancer?" Janie asked.

"You'd better believe it, Janie! But that is another story for another time," Janie's mother said, as the auctioneer appeared in the auctioneer's ring below them to start the auction.

And after that, things grew quiet; and the fun began!

And horse after horse was brought into the auction ring; and Janie's parents looked at one another and at Janie as the auction proceeded, to see Janie's reaction to each horse. And Janie just kept staring straight ahead as if she was waiting for something to happen. Finally, Janie looked up at her parents, breaking her stare.

"In case you're wondering," she whispered. "I'm waiting."

"Why are you waiting?" Janie's father whispered back.

"I'm waiting for a horse to choose me," Janie answered, ever so softly.

Janie's dad shook his head, bewildered.

"Can a horse choose its owner?" Janie's dad whispered to Janie's mother.

"You'd better believe it," Janie's mother whispered back.

And then the horse that would soon be Janie's horse entered the auction ring.

CHAPTER FOURTEEN
THE BIDDING PROCESS

"That's the one!" Janie exclaimed in a whisper, so as to not encourage other would-be bidders to raise their bids. "Did you see how that horse looked right at me? I saw that horse when we walked past the stalls earlier! It was looking at me then, the exact same way!"

"Maybe she has something wrong with her eyes," Janie's father told her jokingly, but lovingly.

Janie shrugged her shoulders.

"You said *this* horse would be *my* horse, and that I could choose! And that's the horse I want," Janie told her father, as the bidding for the horse opened.

"She's a fine-looking young thoroughbred mare," Janie's mother softly said.

"I hope we can afford her," her father interjected as he raised his auction paddle at two hundred dollars, and his bid was immediately matched by a three-hundred-dollar bid.

The Horses of Griffin Farm

Janie's father sat waiting for the bidding to slow down before raising his paddle again.

"I'm not going to get into a bidding war," he said. "Let's see where this thing is going?"

Janie took a deep breath and looked up at her father, as he intently studied the bidding.

"I really do want that horse," she whispered.

And then the bidding slowed and seemed to come to a stop.

And just as the auctioneer was about to call the winning bid, Janie's dad raised his paddle and shouted, "Eight hundred dollars!"

And the auctioneer, after calling for additional bids, and after which there were no further bids, announced, "The bid is for eight hundred dollars! Are there any further bids?" And then after a short pause he shouted out to the anticipating crowd, 'Calling once! Calling twice! Calling three times! Sold to the man in the plaid shirt for eight hundred dollars!"

And then Janie jumped to her feet in excitement, and she threw her hands into the air and shouted out in glory, "Yes! Yes! Yes!"

And the rest would soon become history!

And as impatient as Janie was, she knew she had to wait as Janie's father headed off to pay for the horse. And once the bill of sale and the horse's papers were procured, Janie ran to the horse trailer to fetch a bridle and lead, and her parents headed for the horse's stall.

The Horses of Griffin Farm

The horse pawed the ground impatiently, obviously ill at ease, as Janie's parents stood next to its stall, a pipe corral pen, waiting for Janie to appear. And surprisingly, once Janie appeared at the pen, the anxious horse became calm.

And so . . . Janie climbed atop the final rung of the pipe corral, the horse walked over to her, and bowed its head; and then Janie placed the bridle and lead on the horse, and jumped down from the pipe corral, leaving the lead dangling from the bridle.

As if the horse knew where she was going now, she walked over to the stall opening and waited for the auctioneer's ranch hand to open the stall for Janie.

"I've never seen anything like this," he said, as he picked up the end of the lead and handed it to Janie. "It looks like this is a match made in heaven!"

Janie smiled.

"We chose each other," she told the attendant.

"And luckily, I had enough money in the bank to afford it!" Janie's dad quipped as they walked toward their truck and trailer, horse in tow, guided (of course) by Janie!

"And . . . no . . . you cannot ride in the back of the trailer with the horse," Janie's mother told Janie, anticipating what Janie was about to ask. "We will be home with the horse soon enough."

"But I *can* sleep with her, right?" Janie asked. "You *did* say I could sleep with her during her quarantine."

The Horses of Griffin Farm

"Yes," her mother told her. "A promise is a promise!"

And once the horse was secured in the horse trailer, the three of them and the new horse headed off for home, and for the horse it was a new family and a new herd, of which Janie and her mother and father would quickly become an integral part.

CHAPTER FIFTEEN
THE RIDE HOME

The ride home was basically an uneventful one, except for the occasional thumping of the new horse that came from the new horse banging and pawing the trailer as it was towed behind their truck.

"I hope she's okay," Janie said, as the thumping grew more intense.

Janie's dad turned up the truck's radio to block out the sound.

"I'm sure she'll be fine," he said. "The only other choice is to ride her home," he joked.

"I could do that!" Janie exclaimed, smiling.

"Oh, no!" Janie's mother turned and told her daughter, who was sitting, buckled by her seatbelt into the back seat of the dual cab. "You can't do that! You can barely find yourself out of a paper bag! And it's a long way to home."

"Now, whatever would I be doing inside of a paper bag?" Janie asked.

"Don't get smart with me," her mother told her. "Remember when you got lost at the mall?"

"I was five years old," Janie told her mother. "And that was a long time ago."

"Well, it's not a long enough time for me to let you ride that horse all the way home," Janie's mother told her. "And it might not be good for the horse. What if she has an ulcer or something and needs to rest to get better?"

"I'm sorry. I didn't think about that," Janie said, somewhat apologetically.

"When it comes to horses, or for that matter when it comes to any of the living creatures of this earth, we need to think of the whole picture," Janie's mother told her.

"Do you mean like global warming?" Janie asked.

"That's a big part of the picture," Janie's mother told her. "In fact, it just may be the entire picture."

Janie agreed.

"Why are people the way they are about things?" Janie asked. "I don't understand why people want so much, when all a horse wants is to be a part of the herd."

"Maybe people aren't as smart as horses," Janie's father interjected. "Maybe everyone needs to learn to become a part of the herd."

Janie nodded her head, as her father changed the subject.

The Horses of Griffin Farm

"I do believe we got a good price on this mare," he said. "And she came with papers to boot! I didn't expect that!"

"Eight hundred dollars isn't cheap," Janie's mother protested. "The horses in the slaughter pens in Texas are selling for forty-nine cents a pound! If the average weight of a horse is a thousand pounds, that means horses sent to Texas slaughter pens are being picked up for a mere four hundred and ninety dollars. And that means people can buy a horse from a Texas slaughter pen, bring it here and possibly sell it for double what they paid for it in Texas."

"How do you know all that stuff?" Janie asked.

"I looked it up on the internet," Janie's Mother explained. "And I did the math," Janie's mother added wryly. "I may as well use my math degree for something," she added with a smile.

"It's sad, when people take a horse to a slaughterhouse pen to be sold, especially since the horses go for meat and for other purposes to foreign countries where their uses for those purposes are still legal," Janie's dad interjected.

"Well, I guess at least *we're* in the business of saving horses when we buy them at auction," Janie told her parents. "It's just too bad we can't save them all."

"It's too bad we can't afford to buy *and* feed them all," Janie's mother added.

"Maybe we should go to Texas and buy them all up out of the Texas slaughterhouse pens," Janie said, with great thought and concern after thinking about it for what seemed like only a moment.

"I don't think that would be very practical considering transportation and travel costs, not to mention the time and effort it would take to go all the way to Texas," Janie's father interjected.

"Well then," Janie said, with great determination in her voice, "I'm just going to pretend that this horse came from Texas, was brought here, and was saved from slaughter! And I'm just going to hope no one ever took this horse, or any horse, to be sold from a slaughterhouse pen to be taken to some foreign country to be sold for meat!"

"Just remember you can't believe everything you read on the internet, and that there's a lot of conflicting information about a lot of things out there," Janie's father said, as they veered off the highway and onto a side rode.

"I'm just glad to have a great horse!" Janie told her father, And not too long after that, they arrived home.

CHAPTER SIXTEEN
A Rose By Any Other Name

The horses in barn two had been moved earlier to pasture for the day, as was the usual process for all of the horses when it was warm and sunny; and (as it had been decided earlier) the newly procured auction mare would be moved into the quarantine stall at the far back of barn two, behind the bales of alfalfa shipped in from California as soon as Janie, her parents, and the new mare arrived home.

Janie's parents grew their own round bales of oat hay on the farm, of course; but the alfalfa was gingerly ordered and then used when a horse was ailing or suffering from ulcers or other ailments, because Janie's mother had heard it might help in the healing of a sick horse, because alfalfa was higher in protein; and believing that, she thought it would more than likely help an ailing horse.

The horses at pasture for the day would be brought in at sundown, as was the usual course of procedure on the farm; but this time it appeared Janie's mother and father would have to handle that without Janie's help, because Janie's mother knew Janie more than likely would not want to leave her newly acquired horse.

"We'll get the vet out here as soon as possible," Janie's mother told Janie, as she and Janie unloaded the horse and led it back to the quarantine stall, and as Janie's father went into the house to call the vet for an appointment.

"You'll get a full check up!" Janie promised the horse. "And if anything is wrong with you, we'll make sure you get healed and are as right as rain as soon as possible!"

Ironically, the horse (at least as far as Janie was concerned) seemed to understand exactly what Janie was saying.

As the horse was placed into the quarantine stall at the back of barn two, Janie told her mother, just as her mother had expected, "I'm not going to leave her here in the barn alone."

"I understand," her mother told her. "I'll bring you something to eat and your sleeping bag and pillow, so you won't go hungry, and so you can sleep out here comfortably amongst the hay."

Janie looked up at her mother and smiled.

"I *completely* understand," Janie's mother quickly added. "I spent many a night in the barn back home in California."

"Do you miss California?" Janie asked, as she sat down cross-legged on the hay randomly scattered in front of the quarantine pen.

"Not at all," Janie's mother told her. "I'm exactly where I should be . . . right here in Virginia with you and your father."

The Horses of Griffin Farm

Janie smiled, as her mother turned to exit the barn.

"I'll be right back," Janie's mother said.

And Janie knew her mother wouldn't be gone long.

And, of course, Janie was correct! And before she knew it, her mother was back with a sandwich and a healthy boxed drink, some potato chips, and two apples . . . one for Janie and one for the new horse.

"What should we call this horse?" Janie asked, as she helped her mother spread the sleeping bag out upon the scattered hay in front of the stall, and her mother fluffed Janie's pillow.

Janie took a bite of her apple, and she gave the other apple to her new horse, prior to eating her sandwich and potato chips; and she placed her boxed drink and sandwich and potato chips atop her pillow, waiting for a response to her question about what they should name the new horse.

"Well," her mother finally said, "the horse did come with papers; and her name happens to be on those papers . . ."

"It is? Really? Janie asked. "Then . . . what is her name?"

"Her name is Cheery Day, Janie," Janie's mother told her. "So, what do you think of that name?"

Janie smiled.

"I couldn't *ever* think of a better name for her!" Janie exclaimed. "It's *absolutely* perfect!"

"And why is that?" Janie's mother asked.

"Isn't it obvious?" Janie told her mother. "She brings cheer to my day! And she brought cheer to me today!"

And Janie's mother smiled. And that was because what Janie had just told her was absolutely true!

CHAPTER SEVENTEEN
A Beautiful Morning!

The next morning when Janie's mother went to fetch her from the barn for breakfast, she discovered Janie had moved herself (sleeping bag, pillow and all) from the outside of the quarantine pen to the inside of the pen where Janie was curled up next to the horse, sleeping bag, pillow and all, sound asleep. And that was exactly where Janie's mother found Janie for several days thereafter.

"It's a good thing it's summer break, or you'd be late for school!" Janie's mother told her, as Janie opened her eyes, startled by her mother's entrance into the barn.

"Is it morning already?" Janie asked.

"Yes, it is," Janie's mother told her. "And you have chores to do! So, you'd better get up, have breakfast, and get started on those chores!"

"Okay! Okay! Okay!" Janie said, as she rubbed her eyes and rose to her feet.

The Horses of Griffin Farm

The horse followed suit.

Janie quickly hugged her new horse and said, "Now, don't you worry, Miss Cheery Day! I'll eat my breakfast and be right back with some breakfast for you!"

And then, Janie followed her mother out of the barn and up to the house where scrambled eggs, toast and orange juice were quickly placed on everyone's plates and were just as quickly devoured!

"You'd better change your clothes and head off for your work in the city!" Janie's mother told Janie's father, as he rose to his feet, dressed in his farm gear.

"Oh, no need for that today, or for the remainder of the week!" Janie's father announced. "I'm taking one of my vacation weeks! I thought it was best considering we are welcoming a new member into our herd."

Janie and her mother laughed.

"Well, I sure can use the extra help," Janie's mother said. "I pretty much have my hands full with all these mouths around here to feed."

And then it was Janie's dad's turn to laugh.

"But why didn't you tell me you were taking the week off?" Janie's mother asked.

"Oh, I just thought I would spring a little surprise on you," Janie's father told her.

The Horses of Griffin Farm

And as soon as Janie was finished eating her breakfast, she finished her chores; and then, she kept her promise to Cherry Day, and she returned to Cheery Day's side, and she fed and watered her new horse.

"I love you Miss Cheery Day," she told the horse, as she filled the horse's feeding trough.

And Cheery Day knew what Janie was telling her was true. And she *also* knew she had found her forever home with this girl called Janie.

CHAPTER EIGHTEEN
THE PERFECT HORSE

Now, while it is preferable to have a horse examined and tried out for soundness prior to purchase, such things are simply not viable or practical when a horse is purchased at auction, at least this was the case at this particular horse auction. And the general rule of thumb and understanding at any livestock auction where purchase is made is quite simply, 'buyer beware!'

(And there are many livestock auctions of all sorts in farm country.)

However, for those who were out to rescue animals, this was not a primary concern. And this was most certainly not any sort of a concern at all for Janie, because she had fallen madly in love with her new horse and couldn't wait to not only ride her, but also to 'try her out' in the show ring, and perhaps win a blue ribbon, or even multiple blue ribbons as a hunter jumper champion!

The Horses of Griffin Farm

Of course, Janie had won her share of ribbons in the hunter jumper horse ring; however, with this horse named Cheery Day, things felt and seemed a little different somehow. It was something Janie couldn't explain, because it was only a feeling. But she just knew that Cheery Day and she were meant to accomplish something very big! Janie simply just didn't know what or when, or even how, this would come to be. She just knew in her heart it *would* be!

"This horse is going to be a great hunter jumper champion," Janie told the vet, not doubting and not questioning or wondering about it, as she and her parents observed the veterinarian's examination of Cheery Day later that week.

"I dare say she will be!" the vet told Janie, as he did a cursory examination of the horse's eyes and teeth and proceeded with and examination of the horse's stomach, back, and legs.

"What do you think?" Janie's mother asked, as the vet did a blood draw.

"I'll get the blood test results back in a few days and let you know; but all in all, I would say you have a very fine young horse here," the vet said, as he took out his tools and proceeded to float the horse's teeth. "She's quite sound and attentive," he added. "And I'll dare to say I bet Janie *really* likes her!" he added with a wink, as he turned to see Janie's reaction to his comment.

"I do! I really do" Janie told the vet. "I just *love* this horse!"

The Horses of Griffin Farm

And when the veterinarian's examination was finished, and after he returned to his truck and left to go back to his office, Janie began the now daily grooming of her horse. (They did, after all, choose each other.)

"You are going to have the shiniest coat a horse could ever have!" Janie told Cheery Day. "And you are the very best horse a girl could ever have!" she added, as she gave Cheery Day one great big, huge hug.

And then, Janie set down the horse brush, and she went into the farmhouse to grab a couple of apples, one for her and one for Miss Cheery Day.

The world was full of promise!

CHAPTER NINETEEN
THE TRAINING BEGINS

Before they knew it, Cheery Day was veterinarian cleared, all vaccinations and other procedures were up to date, and Cheery Day was introduced to and integrated into the herd of the horses of Griffin Farm. And because it was now summer, Janie spent every night she possibly could in that barn with her most perfect horse.

Training Cheery Day was more like fun than work, as Janie's mother (an experienced horsewoman in both hunter jumper and western rider style) set up practice jumps for Janie and her horse, and also brought in an outside trainer due to the fact Janie's mother felt it was much better to have an independent source in charge of the training so as to not cause any conflict with her daughter over this or that. (Because as we all know, girls will be girls, just as boys will be boys.)

The Horses of Griffin Farm

And so, Janie's mother hired Mrs. Carter to help with the training; and the choice of Mrs. Carter was because Mrs. Carter was no pushover for either horse or rider.

To say that Mrs. Carter was one tough woman was not an understatement. Not only was she fully trained in all equestrian aspects of horse training, but she had also trained many of the best competitors and their horses in and for various equestrian competition types. She, herself, had been a fierce competitor in several events early on in her life; and her experience in the world of horses had culminated with a long stint as a trick rider on a traveling rodeo circuit, a fact that fascinated young Janie. (But, of course, the rodeo stint only continued until Mrs. Carter ended up having a terrible accident that left her walking with a cane.)

"This horse has great promise," Mrs. Carter told Janie's mother and father, after having observed and made her own physical, as well as observational, evaluation of the horse in and out of the ring, with and without Janie. "And Janie shows great promise as well," she added.

And so, it was decided that a thorough training of both rider and horse should begin, and so it began. And Mrs. Carter let Janie choose into what field of competition Janie and Cheery Day should go, as Janie was young, but was not a complete novice when it came to competing in the horse ring.

The Horses of Griffin Farm

"I want to do hunter jumper with her," Janie told Mrs. Carter. "I like western, but I think I like hunter jumper more," Janie added.

And Janie's mother was just grateful that Janie didn't choose rodeo trick riding to follow in Mrs. Carter's footsteps, even though she had once voiced an interest in joining the circus for many of the same reasons Mrs. Carter had chosen to go on the rodeo circuit.

And so, the training began!

And the training went quickly and beautifully; and even though Janie had competed on other horses with other trainers, this time everything seemed different. It was as though when Janie was riding Cheery Day, that they were one. And the horse seemed to anticipate exactly what needed to be done, almost as though the horse was leading the rider, instead of the other way around.

And this was a fact that did not go unnoticed by Janie's mother or by Mrs. Carter.

"This horse has obviously had extensive training," Mrs. Carter told Janie's mother, as Janie dismounted the horse after their very first training session. "I can only wonder why the previous owners sent her to auction."

"She had some issues early on with ulcers," Janie's mother told Mrs. Carter. "But they were quickly and easily treated."

"My guess is she didn't click with her previous owners, and that they demanded too much from her. But she and Janie are like a

The Horses of Griffin Farm

match made in heaven," Mrs. Carter told Janie's mother, to which Janie's mother nodded her head in agreement.

"They do seem like a good match," Janie's mother said ponderously, as she and Mrs. Carter watched Janie remove the English style saddle from the horse, along with the bridle and bit, and proceeded to the cool down process.

After that, Janie led Cheery Day to the pasture to rejoin the herd. And Janie returned to her mother and Mrs. Carter.

CHAPTER TWENTY
THE DEAL

Janie had so much fun training with Cheery Day (and training Cheery Day) that the days passed quickly. And Mrs. Carter had so much fun training the happy horse and rider duo, that she couldn't seem to stay away! There was just something about these two.

"I have a feeling about Janie and Cheery Day," she told Janie's mother at one late afternoon practice at the ranch. "I mean, I see more than merely talent in these two. I see a passion. And I'd like to make you an offer."

"We can't afford much more in the way of paying you," Janie's mother told Mrs. Carter, as she watched Janie and her horse go over the series of jumps set out for them in the practice ring.

"Well, then . . ." Mrs. Carter began, "I do believe we can come to an understanding; because what I would like to do is to come out here to the ranch three times a week, and perhaps even more often, at no charge to you."

The Horses of Griffin Farm

"Oh, I can't let you do that," Janie's mother told Mrs. Carter. "It just wouldn't be right."

"Look," Mrs. Carter then told Janie's mother, "it really is no problem for me to drive out here in my truck afternoons after I'm finished coaching at the arena. And you have done a good thing rescuing this horse."

"Are you sure you want to give up your time to do this?"

"I'm sure," Mrs. Carter said with determination. "But I will expect you to feed and water me," she added, laughingly.

And then, when the lesson was over, Janie did her usual warm down with Cheery Day.

And when Janie's mother tried to pay Mrs. Carter for the lesson that day, Mrs. Carter refused payment.

"I thought we had an agreement," she told Janie's mother, as Janie and Cheery Day began walking back to Cheery Day's stall. "So, you'd better put that checkbook away and think about what we're all having for dinner tonight!"

Janie's mother smiled. And the reason for her smile was simple. The foremost equestrian trainer had chosen Janie and Cheery Day, just as Janie and Cheery Day had chosen one another that day at the horse auction.

The opportunities seemed limitless, and that's because they probably were limitless!

The Horses of Griffin Farm

"I hope pot roast, green beans and Mashed potatoes and gravy are okay," Janie's mother told Mrs. Carter. "Oh, and I have some apple pie ala mode planned for dessert!" she quickly added.

"And . . . I knew I would be getting the better part of this deal," Mrs. Carter laughed, as she steadied herself on her cane as they walked back to the farmhouse. But I must insist on helping you peel those potatoes!"

And, of course, Janie's mother laughed.

"Are you sure you're getting the better part of this deal?" she asked.

"I'm sure," Mrs. Carter told her. "I'm quite sure."

CHAPTER TWENTY-ONE

Blue Ribbons & Strawberry Rhubarb Pie

It wasn't too long after those first equestrian lessons had started with Mrs. Carter, that the competitions began. And while Janie was being trained in every aspect of equestrian showing, hunter jumper was where her interests had started and stayed; and so, as Mrs. Carter had predicted, and as the summer proceeded, Janie and Cheery Day quickly became the stars of the circuit and the ones to beat.

Janie fastened her blue ribbons to a bulletin board her father had mounted on the wall, along with an eight by ten photo of herself sitting atop her beloved Cheery Day. And any excuse she could think of also sent her into the barn to sleep alongside her beloved horse.

Dinner became a regular event for Mrs. Carter and Janie and her family.

"I'm running out of new things on my 'to cook' list to cook," Janie's mother told Mrs. Carter as their early dinner began one late afternoon, as she set a large serving plate of piping hot, southern fried chicken on the table, next to some mashed potatoes, a bowl of chicken gravy, a bowl of peas and carrots, and a good-sized bowl of homemade whole-berry cranberry sauce.

"That's okay," Mrs. Carter told her. "Just start over from the beginning of the list once the list's end is reached."

And as to that, everyone at the table laughed.

"Dig in!" Janie's father announced.

And that was exactly what everyone did.

Since it was mid-summer now in Virginia, the days were long, and because Janie used any and every excuse possible to be with and to take a ride on her beloved horse, she made an announcement of sorts.

"I think I'll take Cheery Day on an explore," she said. "She's been working very hard; and all the animals have been fed, so why not? It will be good for her! Right, Mrs. Carter?"

Mrs. Carter lowered her eyes and put her napkin to her lips.

"I don't want to get into the middle of anything," she said. "And so, while that sounds very nice, I do believe the answer to that question is up to your mother and your father."

Janie's parents looked at one another and smiled between partaking of mouths of food.

"Well, what do you think, Mother?" Janie's father asked.

"I think it's okay," Janie's mother said. "But I do want to make sure all the rules are followed."

The Horses of Griffin Farm

"I'll take one of the dogs with me for protection," Janie said reassuringly. "And I'll keep my cell phone in my shorts' pocket. And I'll have my trusty whistle around my neck just in case I run into any trouble," she added.

"And you'll be back before it gets dark?" Janie's mother asked, because even though Janie had gone on explores in the past all by herself with Cheery Day and with one (or another) of the dogs, she had never traveled out of the sight of her parents this close to sundown.

"I'll head back to the house as soon as the sun starts to set," Janie promised her now somewhat skeptical mother.

"And I'll stay right here at the farmhouse until you return safely," Mrs. Carter added, knowing Janie was never one to back down when she wanted to do anything.

"You are just like your Swedish great grandmother on my mother's side!" Janie's mother told Janie.

"What do you mean by that?" Janie asked, as she got up from the kitchen table and put her glass, and her dinner plate, and her eating utensils into the dishwasher.

"What I mean by that is that your great grandmother on my mother's side never backed down from anything she made up her mind to do!"

"Hmm," Janie mused, as she checked to make sure her mobile phone was still in her pocket, and as she headed out the back door to go in the direction of the barn where Cheery Day remained in her stall,

The Horses of Griffin Farm

"I guess I *am* like my great grandmother on your mother's side!" she shouted out to her mother, as she began her exit out the back door.

"Just don't abuse it!" Janie's mother yelled after her. "Your grandmother accomplished a lot, but she was also a very safe and careful person so . . ."

"So, be safe!" Janie's father interjected with a shout, as the kitchen back door slammed behind Janie.

"I guess she didn't want any dessert," her mother said. "And you know what that means!"

"It means more strawberry rhubarb pie for the three of us!" Janie's father exclaimed.

And . . . later on, as the rest of the dinner plates, glasses and utensils were removed from the table, Janie's mother brought out the strawberry rhubarb pie and set the table for after dinner coffee and pie (with some help from Janie's father) and the three of them drank their after-dinner coffees and ate heartily of strawberry rhubarb pie!

CHAPTER TWENTY-TWO
THE EXPLORE BEGINS

Janie headed to the barn to fetch Cheery Day, and on the way to Cheery Day's stall, she grabbed her cowboy hat from where it hung on a nail, and she took off her flip flops, that had previously replaced her English style riding boots, and put her sockless feet into her favorite red cowgirl boots, after taking them from where they had leaned against the barn wall underneath the nail where her cowboy hat had previously hung. Then she grabbed Cheery Day's bitless bridle from where it was still hanging from a wardrobe hook next to where her cowboy hat had hung.

"Mrs. Carter has taught me well," Janie thought to herself, as she headed straight to Cheery Day.

It was quick and simple to place the bitless bridle on Cheery Day and then to mount the horse bareback.

The Horses of Griffin Farm

"I think this is one of my most favorite ways to ride," Janie thought to herself as she rode Cheery Day bareback out of the open barn door and headed off for her explore.

Janie's mobile phone remained in her pocket, and the whistle on a string around her neck remained safely in its proper place.

"Better safe than sorry," Janie thought, as she felt her chest to assure herself that the whistle was still there.

Then Janie called out to the dog that guarded the barn (Pinkerton) so that the dog would not only follow her, but so that the dog would also be her protector . . . just in case there was an unexpected emergency on the trail as she rode; however, she was also confident that would not be the case.

And then the three of them, Janie, Cheery Day, and Pinkerton (the dog) set out on the explore.

"Janie's mother looked out the kitchen window.

"I wonder where she'll be exploring today?" she asked, as if talking to herself.

"Well, I will bet you dollars to donuts she's heading to the far end of our property to give the forest an explore," Janie's father said, answering the question that wasn't actually asked.

"Is it safe?" Janie's mother scowled, thinking perhaps Janie should not have headed out for an explore after all, considering how late it was in the day.

"That girl can take care of herself," Mrs. Carter interjected. "She reminds me a bit of myself at that age."

Janie's mother took a deep breath.

"I'm going to assume you're right," Janie's mother told Mrs. Carter. "But I'm afraid we'll just have to wait and see."

And then, as Janie rode out to the far backside of the property toward the forest, Janie's mother wrung her hands in despair.

"She's been in the forest before," Janie's father said. "So, please don't worry, Mother."

"But she's never gone there so late in the day, Father. We should have never let her go riding this late in the afternoon," Janie's mother told Janie's father.

"Well, she's gone a little too far out there now for us to stop her," Janie's father replied.

And after that, they (all three of them) decided that they just needed to trust Janie and that everything would turn out just fine. Because, after all, Janie was living in a fairytale, and fairytales always had happy endings.

CHAPTER TWENTY-THREE

A STOP BY THE STREAM

As Janie, Cheery Day and Pinkerton entered the forested area at the back of Griffin Farm, Janie had no idea what to expect, even though this wasn't the first time she'd explored the forest. Although she knew she might encounter a deer or two, or perhaps even a wolf, Janie was fearless! After all, Janie and her mother had gone well into the depths of the forest to gather wild raspberries for canning many, many times. So, how dangerous could a ride through the forest be? Besides, most of the forest was on their land, uncleared (of course) and would remain so as a protective area of sorts for the wildlife that had presumedly always lived there prior to settlers of the area long ago moving onto the property.

"Keeping the forest as it is now, is the least that we can do," Janie's mother explained to Janie one spring day, as the two of them gathered wild raspberries for jam. "We need to share this earth with all of the creatures that exist upon it with us. That's what we are *really*

The Horses of Griffin Farm

meant to do when the Bible tells us we have dominion over the creatures of the earth."

Janie remembered her mother's words as she stopped by the familiar stream she often visited on her explores. And knowing both Cheery day and Pinkerton were probably thirsty (since it was a very warm day) she gave Cheery Day the signal to lower her neck, which Cheery Day did in order to enable Janie to slide down Cheery Day's neck to the ground (an old rodeo trick Mrs. Carter had taught Cheery Day that was most convenient).

Since Cheery Day was wearing a bridle that had no bit, she was able to drink and nibble on the wild grasses next to the stream; and Pinkerton drank his fill of the stream's water, as Janie gathered bunches of mid-summer wildflowers to bring back to the house for her mother and Mrs. Carter.

Janie motioned for Cheery Day to lower her neck once again, and Janie carefully placed the wildflowers under the top left side strap of Cheery Day's bitless bridle.

And then Janie heard something. Cheery day raised her head and bristled, and Pinkerton went running in the direction of the sound.

Could it be? It sounded like the muffled cries of a child.

And so, Janie gave the command for Cheery Day to lower her head once again; and Janie climbed up Cheery Day's neck to a seated position atop her horse and called out for Pinkerton, who quickly returned to Cheery Day's side.

The Horses of Griffin Farm

The three of them ventured through the forest in the direction of the sound. It was a cry for help, and Janie knew she had to do something. She took her mobile phone from her pocket and called 911, and she explained the situation. The dispatcher at the other end of the call traced Janie's exact position through the police dispatcher's GPS tracer, and Janie was assured help was on the way.

"Better tell them to either bring some horses, or to get some horses from my mother and father at Griffin Farm," Janie whispered into her mobile phone.

And then, she called her parents and Mrs. Carter, who all at that exact moment, just happened to be sitting in the living room, each finishing a second cup of coffee as they watched the widescreen TV and heard a breaking news report about a missing child, a young girl from the area, who was believed to have been kidnapped and for which an all-points bulletin had been announced.

And then the sounds of sirens were heard coming from outside the farmhouse; and when the sirens abruptly stopped, they heard a sharp knock at the front door. Janie's dad went to the front door of the farmhouse and opened it. It was the local sheriff and his posse. They had acted quickly on Janie's call to 911, and they needed some horses.

It seemed that in the search for the missing child, they had developed a viable lead.

CHAPTER TWENTY-FOUR
Amongst The Trees IN The Forest

Janie and Cheery Day followed Pinkerton, the dog, into the forest toward the sound Janie had first heard at their stop by the stream. And as they got closer to the sound, the source of it was obvious. It was (indeed) a child, calling out to them in muffled screams. And soon they would find out why the screams sounded muffled.

And Janie did as she was taught; and she even looked for landmarks as she rode through the forest, even though she assumed both Cheery Day and Pinkerton would more than likely know the way back to the farmhouse.

Cheery Day was resolute in her search for the source of the cries in the forest, only stopping for a moment when startled by a bird flying too close to her eyes.

And because this portion of this particular patch of Virginia forest was seemingly untouched and remained as it always was prior to the days when farming and logging had mostly changed Virginia's landscape, this forest was filled with tall, old angiosperm trees of oak, maple, and ash. And it's inherited indigenous beauty had never gone unnoticed by Janie.

And as the birds chased the insects and sang their songs among the rustling leaves of the trees, the threesome proceeded onward in the search for the calls of seeming distress. And not after too long, an unfamiliar and very surprising clearing of sorts was discovered amidst the rather dense forest of mostly untouched trees.

You see, there in the center of a nearly perfect circular clearing with a diameter of approximately thirty feet, stood one very old and very large oak tree.

Pinkerton, the dog, immediately ran toward the far side of the old tree, the side that could not be seen from Janie's perspective as she sat where she was at that time atop Cheery Day. Pinkerton came out from behind the tree and barked at Janie and Cheery Day, running forward and back from the tree, beckoning them toward the tree.

And so, Janie directed Cheery Day to go to the old oak tree with a quick kick of her red cowgirl boots, and off they bounded toward the tree in the center of the clearing.

Once there, Cheery Day quickly lowered her head to the ground, and Janie slid down Cheery Day's neck in quick descent. Time was of the essence, because right there, tied to the tree, was a child, a young girl, her mouth gagged and muzzled with a dirty cloth, tied at the back of her neck.

The Horses of Griffin Farm

Fearlessly, Janie first untied and removed the dirty cloth from the child's mouth.

"Move quickly," the child whispered. "The old man may be back soon."

Janie reassured the child help was coming as she removed the small, Swiss army knife from her pocket, and cut through the ropes that bound the girl to the old oak tree.

The girl attempted to shed the dirt, dust, and leaves from the dress she was wearing with her hands, as Cheery Day lowered her head once again, and Janie helped the young girl first onto Cheery Day's neck, and then up onto Cheery Day's back.

Make room for me!" Janie told the young girl. "And when I get up there on the horse, hold on tightly to my waist, and don't let go! And don't fall! We'll be moving out of here as fast as we can go!"

The frightened, young girl nodded her head as Janie mounted Cheery Day.

And then . . . they heard the rustling of leaves.

"It's the old man!" the young girl screamed, as an old, white haired, bearded man appeared in the clearing amongst the forest trees where he had held the young girl captive, gagged, and muzzled with a dirty rag and bound by ropes to the old oak tree in the clearing in the forest he alone had created.

The Horses of Griffin Farm

"He has a shotgun!" the girl screamed, as Pinkerton, the dog, rushed at the old, bearded man, sending him crashing hard onto the ground of the forest clearing.

Taken by surprise, the shotgun flew from the hands of the man, landing some distance away from where he fell. And Pinkerton, being ever protective and diligent, immediately ran to where the shotgun had fallen! And then, as if playing a simple game of fetch the stick (which was a common, everyday game Pinkerton often played with Janie's father) Pinkerton picked up the shotgun with his mouth and teeth, and the three of them, now becoming four, began their run toward the farmhouse!

But that wasn't all that happened. There came a growl from the forest, brought there by a black bear guarding her young cubs; and as the foursome fed the scene, Janie quickly looked behind, and over her shoulder, and Janie saw the old man being taken down by the bear.

"I didn't know there were bears in the forest!" Janie exclaimed, incredulously, as they quickly fled in the direction of the farmhouse, and as the flowers in Cheery Day's bridle flew everywhere in their haste.

And (after that, after all of the excitement) it was a good thing Pinkerton and Cheery Day knew their way home out of the forest; because in all the excitement Janie had forgotten all of the landmarks she had marked in her mind, and she simply couldn't tell the forest from the trees!

CHAPTER TWENTY-FIVE
IN THE CLEARING

Once out of the forest and into the farm clearing, the foursome were met by four sheriff's deputies, armed and mounted upon four of the Griffin Farm horses. As our heroine, her horse and her dog, and her rescued (now forever) young friend approached the deputies, tears ran down both girls' cheeks.

"It's done!" Janie claimed from atop Cheery Day, the young girl holding on to Janie as if her life depended on it.

"I've never been on a horse before this," the young, exhausted girl whispered, simply happy to simply be alive.

And when questioned as to what happened, an exhausted, out of breath Janie merely said. "A bear got the old man. We're all safe now."

One of the deputies remained with the foursome, while the other three deputies went into the forest to see if they could find the old man.

The Horses of Griffin Farm

And when the foursome and the deputy got to the farmhouse where the local sheriff remained waiting for them, Janie and her newly rescued forever friend sat down with the sheriff, Janie's parents, and Mrs. Carter, and the rest of the story unfolded.

The child Janie had rescued was named, 'Hope'.

"What a perfect name for you, my child," Mrs. Carter said.

And then the girl told Mrs. Carter, "I never gave up hoping and praying I would be rescued. And I was rescued! I can't believe I was actually found out there in that forest!"

"Our girl, Janie, is quite remarkable," Mrs. Carter told the girl named 'Hope'.

"Oh, I can't take *all* of the credit for this," Janie interjected. "I couldn't have ever done this without Cheery Day, my horse, and our family's dog, Pinkerton, not to mention the black bear who finally took that evil guy down."

"Did you check to see if he was actually dead?" the sheriff asked Janie.

"Are you kidding me?" Janie asked. "We got out of there as fast as we could go!"

"Well, your dog bringing in the man's shotgun was a nice touch," the sheriff mused, much to Janie's delight.

"I told you I didn't do it alone," Janie told him.

And then Hope's parents were called to come and take her home. Poor little Hope had been held captive for nearly twenty-four hours, taken from daycare and gagged and tied to a tree, and all she could think about was hugging her parents and taking a good hot bubble bath.

Janie's mother and father sat silently as everything unfolded, happy that all was okay, happy that things had turned out as they had turned out, and grateful both girls were safe.

"Were you aware the parents offered a reward for any information relating to the return of their child?" the sheriff asked Janie's parents.

"Well, it wouldn't be our reward," Janie's father told the sheriff, as Janie's mother nodded her head in agreement. "This reward should go to Janie."

"I don't want a reward for me," Janie told the sheriff. I want the reward to go to a horse rescue charity."

"All of it?" the sheriff asked. "It's a twenty-thousand-dollar reward," he added. "And there may be more."

"Why so high? And why could there be more?" Janie's mother asked.

"The initial twenty thousand dollars is coming from Hope's family and friends," the sheriff began, "and even though the bear may have been the one to finally get this guy, the modus operandi explained to us just now by your daughter indicates this may be a serial killer that has been hunted for several years, committing this same crime over several states, beginning with a skeleton found bound with rope to a tree several years ago in the Florida Everglades."

"It's nice to know I did some good," Janie told the sheriff.

"I told you she was a tough kid," Mrs. Carter interjected, as a knock came at the farmhouse door.

It was Hope's parents, excited and happy their child was found safe and alive.

"We expected the worst," Hope's mother said, as Hope ran to her parents.

"She's our only child," Hope's father added.

"Not for long," Hope's mother said, as she looked first down at Hope who was holding on tightly to her pant leg, and then up to Hope's father who stood alongside Hope's mother, very much surprised that he was going to be a father again.

"Do you mean that I'm going to be a big sister?" Hope asked.

"You sure are!" Hope's mother told her.

And as it turned out, the body of the old man was indeed found mauled to death by the black bear in the forest. And he was indeed the wanted serial killer that had been previously at large. And all of the resulting reward money from all of the states in which he had committed his horrendous crimes, with multiple skeletons found therein of young girls, did offer up their rewards. And all of the money went to the various horse and animal rescue centers within those various states, as (according to Janie) it should be given, in honor of

The Horses of Griffin Farm

Cheery Day and Pinkerton, without whom the child named Hope may never have been rescued, and a serial killer may have never been found.

"All's well that ends well," Janie's father said, as they sat down at the dinner table a few days later, after hearing the news about the significance of Hope's rescue and the death of the old man from the sheriff.

"And it all goes to prove that the acorn doesn't fall far from the tree," Mrs. Carter added.

"And what tree is that?" Janie asked. "And who is the acorn? And who is the tree?"

"I can see we have a budding philosopher on our hands," Janie's father told Mrs. Carter.

"Life does carry on," Mrs. Carter said. "So, Janie, I assume that for now we will put your questions on the table to be answered at a later time."

"But where is the table? And when is the time?" Janie asked.

And then, they all laughed as they passed around the serving plates piled high with food.

And, according to Janie's father, the 'roast beast' dinner was delicious!

www.ingramcontent.com/pod-product-compliance
Ingram Content Group UK Ltd.
Pitfield, Milton Keynes, MK11 3LW, UK
UKHW022232230426
12048UKWH00016BA/1206